BEN FRANKLIN'S
BIG SHOCK

BY JUDITH JANGO-COHEN
ILLUSTRATIONS BY KEVIN LEPP

On My Own
SCIENCE

M Millbrook Press/Minneapolis

The author thanks Gretchen Bierbaum, editor, for her expertise and support.

Millbrook Press, Inc.
A division of Lerner Publishing Group
241 First Avenue North
Minneapolis, MN 55401 U.S.A.

Website address: www.lernerbooks.com

Library of Congress Cataloging-in-Publication Data

Jango-Cohen, Judith.
    Ben Franklin's big shock / by Judith Jango-Cohen ; illustrations by Kevin Lepp.
      p.   cm. — (On my own holidays)
    Includes bibliographical references.
    ISBN-13: 978–1–57505–873–3 (lib. bdg. : alk. paper)
    ISBN-10: 1–57505–873–1 (lib. bdg. : alk. paper)
    1. Electricity—Experiments—Juvenile literature. 2. Franklin, Benjamin, 1706–1790—Juvenile literature. 3. Discoveries in science—Juvenile literature. I. Lepp, Kevin, ill. II. Title. III. Series.
QC533.J36 2006
537'.078—dc22   2005010434

Manufactured in the United States of America
2 3 4 5 6 7 – JR – 11 10 09 08 07 06

*To my mother, who helped me with my first book
report about Ben Franklin, and to my father, who,
like Ben, is always up to something*—J.J-C.

*To my Lord, my family, and my friends—your
encouragement brings out my best*—K.L.

Frightening Lightning

Benjamin Franklin dashed outside,
early one Friday in 1752.

A storm was about to pounce on Philadelphia.

Ben wanted to watch.

He headed toward the blue black
clouds above Society Hill.

FLASH!

A jagged claw of lightning slashed two
housetops.

Soon, red flames spurted from the roofs.

Minutes later, firefighters bolted up the hill.
Luckily, Ben had formed Philadelphia's first
fire company sixteen years earlier.

Ben was always up to something.

He had set up the city's police force.

He had opened a lending library.

Now Ben was busy with a scientific project.

He had been studying a kind of
energy called electricity.

Ben did many experiments to learn more.

He became convinced that
lightning was electricity.

Ben wanted to test this idea.

People had many ideas about lightning.
Some thought lightning was a weapon
that God hurled when angry.
Other people believed that evil spirits
made the lightning.
During a storm, people climbed
to the top of church steeples.
They rang the church bells
to scare away the spirits.
Sadly, tall towers were dangerous places.
Lightning often struck,
killing the bell ringers.
Many scientists shared Ben's belief
that lightning was electricity.
But no one had thought of a way to prove it.
Ben Franklin set out to solve the mystery.

The Mysteries of Electricity

Swarms of people buzzed around
Ben Franklin's house.
They nudged and shoved.
Everyone wanted to see inside.
There were flickering flashes.
There were lots of pops like pistol shots.
SNAP! FIZZLE–FLASH! CRACK!
What was Ben Franklin up to?

Ben was experimenting with electricity.
In the 1700s, there was much to learn.
People had not yet discovered how to use
electric energy to power machines.
People cooked their food over a fire.

Candles or oil lamps lit their homes,
instead of electric lightbulbs.
But scientists knew how to create electricity.
To make electricity, Ben spun a glass globe.
The twirling globe rubbed against a cloth.
This rubbing created an electric charge.
Ben stored the charge in a glass-and-metal
bottle called a Leyden jar.

Using the Leyden jar,

Ben performed tricks with electricity.

Curious neighbors watched as Ben gave

himself flyaway hair.

When he touched the jar, a charge went

through his body to the tips of his hair.

But electricity meant more than

magic tricks to Ben.

It was the most exciting subject

he had ever studied.

Ben wanted to understand what electricity

was and how it worked.

Ben invented more experiments.
He carefully watched what happened.
Then Ben found some answers.
Rubbing causes electricity to flow out
of an object and into another.
One object loses some of its electricity.
The other object gains electricity.
Losing or gaining electricity gives
an object an electrical charge.

17

Ben also noticed that electricity flows
easily through some materials.
He called these materials conductors.
Metal and water are good conductors.

Ben discovered that other materials
block or slow the flow of electricity.
Electricity does not travel through
these materials.
It stays mostly on the surface.
Ben called these materials nonconductors.
Glass, wax, feathers, and silk are
nonconductors.

Ben experimented with
different-shaped conductors.
He learned that pointy-tipped
metal was a special conductor.
He put a pointed rod next to
a charged metal ball.
The rod pulled the charge from the ball.
Pointed metal had attracted the electricity
without touching the ball.

From his experiments, Ben put together
a clear picture of how electricity works.
No other scientist had done that.
But Ben was not yet satisfied.
There was another electricity mystery
he wanted to solve.

Ben's Brainstorm

Ben strode through Philadelphia.

His mind was in the clouds.

Ben looked up at the drifting mounds.

How could electricity form in clouds?

Ben imagined winds tossing water droplets.

The droplets bump and rub together.

Electrical charges build up.

Then a blazing flash rips through the air.

Ben felt sure that lightning was a
stupendous electrical spark.

Ben wrote down the ways that
electricity and lightning are alike.
Both give off light.
Both travel swiftly in a crooked direction.
Both can pass through water and metals.
Both make a crack or noise.

Lightning certainly seemed to be electrical.

But how could Ben prove it?

He could not climb up to the clouds.

Maybe he could lure down the lightning.

Ben knew that electric charges
are attracted to pointed metal.

What if he placed a metal-tipped rod
high in a tower?

Could the rod draw charges from the
clouds as it had from the metal ball?

There were no tall towers in Philadelphia.

But a new church was soon to be built.

Perhaps that would have a high steeple.

Ben imagined the rising spire as he

passed the site for the new church.

Then a young boy bumped into him.

The boy was clutching a string.

A paper kite tugged in his hand.

The boy let out the line, and the kite

climbed toward the clouds.

Laughing and patting the boy's head,

Ben hurried home.

He might not need the steeple after all.

Unlocking the Mystery

Ben had always liked kites.
When he was a boy, Ben had
done an experiment with a kite.
He discovered that it could
pull him across a pond.
Now Ben would need a kite to
conduct another experiment.

With two thin strips of cedarwood,

Ben made a cross.

He tied a silk handkerchief to the cross.

A silk kite would bear the rain

and wind better than paper.

To the top of the kite, Ben added

a sharp pointed wire.

Ben tied a line of twine to the kite.

He attached a metal key, a conductor.

He knotted a silk ribbon below the key.

Silk is a nonconductor.

Holding the silk ribbon would

keep the electricity from reaching Ben.

Ben had never been so eager

for a thunderstorm.

Then one summer day in 1752,
smoky clouds choked the sun.
Pelting winds bent tree limbs.
Birds hid in the bushes.
Mothers called their children inside.

Ben grabbed his kite and called to William,
his twenty-one-year-old son.
The two raced through the rain.
People dashing home must have wondered
what Ben Franklin was up to.

Ben and William arrived at a big field.

Ben was glad that no one was around.

He did not want an audience.

If lightning was not electricity,

people would laugh at him

and his experiment.

Ben handed the kite to William.

William ran through the field.

Gusts of wind swept the kite up higher

and higher, tossing and bobbing.

Ben motioned for William to

join him in a nearby shed.

They had to keep the silk ribbon dry.

A soggy ribbon would

conduct electricity.

They could get shocked.

Ben and William watched as a cloud
passed over the kite.
Ben touched his knuckle to the key.
It was cold and dead.
William touched it too.
Nothing!
They waited in the shed, staring at the sky.

Ben was about to reel in his kite.
Then he noticed that loose threads
in the twine were standing on end.
It reminded Ben of his electrified hair.
Ben moved his knuckle toward the key.

ZZZZAP!

Charges flew to his finger.

Ben received only a small shock
from the key.
But a big shock of excitement
surged through him.
He was right!

Taming the Lightning

CRACK!! KABLAM!

A bolt of lightning blasted the Franklin home.

Neighbors hurried over.

The Franklins were safe inside.

There was no fire, thanks to Ben.

He had had yet another idea.

Ben knew that pointy metal attracts

electricity, like lightning.

So he figured out a way to use metal

to protect houses.

In September of 1752, Ben had
attached a metal rod to his chimney.
The nine-foot rod was crowned
with a pointed copper tip.
A wire ran from the base of the rod.
The wire connected to a piece
of metal in the ground.
When lightning struck the
Franklin home, it did not hit the roof.
Instead, it was attracted to the metal rod.
The electricity flowed down the rod,
through the wire, and safely into
the ground.

Ben not only protected his home, he
protected Philadelphia's tallest buildings.
They were the first buildings in the world
to be guarded by lightning rods.
Most people in America and Europe
started using lightning rods.
Many lives were saved, and the rods
came to be called Franklin rods.
Ben's work paved the way for electrical
inventions we still use today.
Meanwhile, he satisfied his curiosity,
had fun, and made the world a safer place.
That is what Ben Franklin was up to.

Afterword

No one knows how Ben Franklin thought of the kite experiment. He never explained how he came up with the idea. Franklin first considered placing a metal point in a high tower. He wrote about this idea to other scientists. French scientists conducted the experiment in May 1752. The experiment proved that lightning was electrical. But letters took months to travel by ship to America. So Franklin knew nothing about this when he flew his kite a bit later. Franklin won great praise for his work with electricity. In 1753, he received the Copley Medal. This was the world's most important scientific award. He even received congratulations from the king of France. Franklin had only two years of formal schooling. Yet he became the most famous scientist in America.

Glossary

charge: a stored amount of electricity

conductor: a material that allows electricity to pass through it easily

electricity: a form of energy that is in everything

experiment: a test to find out if an idea is correct

lightning: a flash of light caused by electricity moving between clouds or between a cloud and the ground

lightning rod: a metal rod placed on top of a building. It conducts electricity away from the building and into the ground.

nonconductor: a material that slows or stops the flow of electricity

Further Reading

Books

Fleming, Candace. *Ben Franklin's Almanac: Being a True Account of the Good Gentleman's Life.* New York: Atheneum Books for Young Readers, 2003.

Giblin, James Cross. *The Amazing Life of Benjamin Franklin.* New York: Scholastic Press, 2000.

Kramer, Stephen. *Lightning!* Minneapolis: Carolrhoda Books, Inc., 1992.

Schanzer, Rosalyn. *How Ben Franklin Stole the Lightning.* New York: HarperCollins Publishers, 2003.

Streissguth, Tom. *Benjamin Franklin.* Minneapolis: Lerner Publications Company, 2005.

CD-Rom

Fritz, Jean. *What's the Big Idea, Ben Franklin?* New York: Scholastic, 1999.

Websites

The Electric Ben Franklin
http://www.ushistory.org/franklin/
This site includes a timeline of Franklin's life, his entire autobiography, a virtual tour of some important locations in Franklin's life, and games and experiments to do at home.

Kids' Lightning Information and Safety
http://www.kidslightning.info/zaphome.htm
Links and information about lightning and how to be safe around lightning are found on this site.

The World of Ben Franklin
http://sln.fi.edu/franklin/
Text and activities provide insight into Ben Franklin's role as a scientist, inventor, statesman, and philosopher.